PIRATES

✦ PIRATES ✦

BY KAREN MCWILLIAMS

FRANKLIN WATTS
NEW YORK/LONDON/TORONTO/SYDNEY
A FIRST BOOK/1989

Samuel Bellamy quote on page 47 from
The Pirates of the New England Coast 1630-1730
by George Francis Dow and John Henry Edmonds,
Argosy-Antiquarian, Ltd., 1923. Reprint 1968.

Photographs courtesy of:
The Granger Collection: pp. 8, 17, 20, 26 (top),
41, 43, 56, 57; New York Public Library Picture
Collection: pp. 11, 15, 16, 19, 23, 26, 29, 36;
Culver Pictures, Inc.: pp. 32 (left), 50, 53, 54;
The Bettmann Archive, Inc.: 32 (right) 37;
Aerial Photography Services, Inc.: p. 35; State
Department of Cultural Resources, Raleigh, N.C.:
p. 39; Steve Pope: 45, 48.

Library of Congress Cataloging-in-Publication Data

McWilliams, Karen.
Pirates / by Karen McWilliams.
p.   cm.   (A First book)
Bibliography: p.
Includes index.
Summary: Describes the ships, social conditions, rules,
and behavior of pirates and includes stories from the lives
of such famous pirates as Blackbeard, Samuel Bellamy,
and the female pirates Mary Read and Anne Bonny.
ISBN 0-531-10464-8
1. Pirates—Juvenile literature. [1. Pirates.] I. Title.
G535.M38   1989
810.4'53—dc19   87-23711   CIP   AC

 CONTENTS

To Jean Tanguay
and Julio Espinosa

THE LIFE OF A PIRATE

"Sail off the starboard bow!" "Man your stations!" "Prepare for boarding!" These are calls that you might hear if you sailed on a British or American pirate ship during the seventeenth or eighteenth centuries.

There have been many movies made about pirates. Movie pirates are men who like nothing better than a good fight at sea. They swing aboard their prey, shooting pistols and clashing *cutlasses.* In no time, the pirates capture the ship that is loaded with gold, silver, and jewels. Later, they bury treasure chests, intending to return for them.

In the movies, pirates leave their prisoners on desert islands to die. Or they tie their hands, blindfold their eyes, and make them "walk the plank." The prisoners usually meet their end by drowning or being eaten by sharks.

PIRATES HAVE BEEN PORTRAYED IN MOVIES AND ON
TELEVISION AS LIKING NOTHING BETTER THAN A GOOD
FIGHT. IN REAL LIFE, THIS WAS NOT ALWAYS TRUE.

Movie pirates are handsome and romantic. They are men who set out to become pirates because of their love of adventure and quest for gold.

In real life, however, few men actually planned to be pirates. Life was hard in those days. The people who were rich were very, very rich and almost everyone else was poor. Many men signed aboard *merchantmen* or warships hoping that they could earn a better living at sea than they would remaining at home.

Life at sea was hard, too. Wages were low. Common sailors often ate spoiled food, while the officers ate the best cuts of meat and the freshest vegetables. Many seamen got sick and died. On some ships, captains punished sailors by beating them with a *cat-o'-nine-tails*. It was no wonder that sailors readily left their ships and signed aboard pirate ships hoping that they would find an easier, richer life.

Pirates all took part in making decisions. They voted on their destinations and who would command their ships. If a pirate captain was unfair or could not perform his duties, he was deposed and another was elected in his place. If men aboard a pirate ship refused to accept the majority's decision, they left and went out on their own.

The captain of a pirate ship was usually the only one on board with a private cabin, but he ate the same food as his men and performed the same duties. Most captains only had complete authority during battle.

The crew also voted for the quartermaster, who was second in command. It was his duty to decide what plunder to keep, supervise the sale of the cargo, and give each man his share.

When signing on to a pirate ship, a person was read the ship's articles and then signed his name, or made his mark (if he couldn't write) to show he was in agreement with them. The articles told how much booty each man was allowed, how much extra was awarded to the wounded, and what punishments were given for breaking rules.

Quarrels between the men were settled by fighting duels on shore. Crimes of murder, stealing, and desertion were tried in a pirate court. If a person was found guilty, he could be thrown overboard, executed by firing squad, lashed forty times with a cat-o'-nine-tails, or marooned on a deserted island with little food

A GALLEON—A SAILING VESSEL USED FOR WAR
OR COMMERCE—OF THE SIXTEENTH CENTURY

and water, a pistol, and gunpowder. Or he could be "keelhauled"—tied up, thrown overboard, and then dragged under the hull of the ship to the other side. Even if he survived, he would have been badly cut by *barnacles* growing on the ship's hull.

Because everyone was treated equally aboard a pirate ship, and there was the chance of becoming very rich, it was fairly easy for pirates to recruit sailors. But not everyone had the desire to become a pirate. At times, pirates forced (or impressed) sailors to come aboard their ship, especially if they had special skills that were needed.

Like all sailors, pirates feared nothing more than fire. On most ships, there were rules about smoking pipes and lighting lanterns and candles. The ships carried barrels of gunpowder, and one stray spark could ignite the powder, causing the ship to explode and sink.

When pirates sighted a possible prey, they followed the ship for hours, sometimes days, to decide if she could be easily captured. Then the pirates hoisted the *Jolly Roger*, the flag with each pirate ship's particular emblem, and fired pistols and muskets at the merchants. Pirate musicians beat their drums and blasted their trumpets. The fiercer the pirates looked, the more likely the merchants would be to surrender. If the merchants showed much resistance, the pirates often retreated.

Sometimes, if a merchantman didn't surrender at that first fierce display, the pirates would *shoot a broadside*. Cannonballs would rip through the merchantman's sails and masts, crippling the ship. Next, the men would throw grappling irons to her rigging, pull the two ships together, and tie them side by side. Then they would swarm aboard.

If the merchantmen did not fight, the pirates took what they wanted, then usually released the sailors unharmed. Some pirates tortured or beat their prisoners if they showed resistance. Some pirates were cruel only to merchants from a particular nation or port they hated.

Pirates would occasionally keep the captured ship. Then they would either take the prisoners aboard their own ship or maroon them on an island, usually giving them food, water, and a pistol. Prisoners were usually marooned where they would be picked up by a passing ship. There is no actual record of pirates making prisoners "walk the plank."

A few pirates captured Spanish or Portuguese *galleons*, which were loaded with gold, silver, and gems from Mexican and South American mines. A pirate's share from one galleon could make him rich for life. Most pirates spent what they made and rarely did anyone bury his treasure.

In 1651, the British passed the first navigation laws stating that the colonists must buy English goods from English ships with English crews and an English captain. In addition, the merchandise was highly taxed. Therefore, most colonists in the West Indies and America welcomed pirates, because they sold quality merchandise for good prices. Also, they were big spenders in town.

A PORTUGUESE GALLEON, USUALLY FILLED WITH GOLD, SILVER, OR GEMS. THESE SHIPS WERE PREYED ON BY PIRATES.

PIRATES DIVIDING UP A TREASURE (PAINTING
BY HOWARD PYLE FROM THE BOOK OF PIRATES).
FEW PIRATES EVER BURIED THEIR TREASURES;
THEY USUALLY SPENT THEIR RICHES.

Pardons were sometimes issued to pirates.
Some stated that the pirate was free from
punishment—if he gave a share of the booty to
the governor. Many governors and business-
men paid for pirate ships and supplies in
return for a share of the plunder.

European governments were very angry
about what was happening in the colonies
between the colonists and pirates. Sometimes
kings sent warships to capture pirates and

bring them to trial. If the pirates were found guilty, they were sentenced to hang. Often their bodies were embalmed in tar, bound with chains, and hung from a *gibbet* to serve as a warning for others not to pursue the life of a pirate.

THIS ENGLISH ENGRAVING SHOWS A PIRATE HANGED AT EXECUTION DOCK IN LONDON IN THE 1700S.

◆2◆

PIRATES, SHIPS, AND JOLLY ROGERS

Before turning pirate, a man could have been a farmer, tailor, writer, surgeon, carpenter, clergyman, *cooper*, or sailor. Most did not want to bring shame upon their respectable families, so they often gave themselves nicknames such as "Blackbeard," "Calico Jack," "Timberhead," "Black Bart," and "Red Hand."

Pirate ships had interesting names, too. Some were named after royalty, such as the *Charles II* and the *King James.* Many had fearsome names, such as the *Sudden Death* and the *Black Joke* or religious names such as the *Merry Christmas* and the *Most Holy Trinity. Revenge* was the most common name given to ships, because some pirates felt they were taking revenge against the wrongs people had done them.

Most pirate ships were captured merchantmen. The men often built up the *gunwales* to

ATTACK ON A GALLEON (BY HOWARD PYLE)

protect themselves during battle. They cut down the deckhouses, so the ships could be easily hidden in lagoons and not be seen by prey. Also, a lighter ship could maneuver at faster speeds.

In warm tropical waters, the hull of a ship quickly became covered with barnacles, which would cling to the wood, and teredo worms would bore holes in the ship's hull. This slowed down vessels and destroyed the wooden planks, causing leaks. Ships, therefore, needed to be *careened* throughout the year.

When pirates were ready to careen their ship, they usually sailed into shallow water in a hidden lagoon so they wouldn't be surprised by enemies.

First, the men unloaded cannons and supplies from the ship. Then they built a camp on

AN ENGRAVING OF A MAN-
OF-WAR, A WARSHIP OF A
RECOGNIZED NAVY (BY FRANS
HUYS AFTER A PAINTING BY
PETER BRUEGEL THE ELDER)

the beach, placing their weapons within reach, in case of attack.

On the ship, the men shifted the cargo and the rest of the gear to one side to expose the hull of the other side. Sometimes they pulled the ship over more by tying ropes from the masts to nearby trees.

The pirates then scraped the barnacles off the exposed hull and replaced planks that were infested with teredo worms. Then they coated the hull with a mixture of tar, tallow, and sulfur. After one side of a ship was completed, the gear and cargo were shifted to the other side and the process was repeated.

While resting from this hard work, the men would amuse themselves by eating, drinking, swimming, and gambling. Sometimes musicians played while everyone sang sea chanteys and tavern songs or danced the hornpipe. Sometimes the men played "pirates' pantomime," also called "mock trial."

Pirates played "mock trial" because everyone was afraid of being captured and brought to trial, and this was practice for the real thing.

In 1721, Captain Charles Johnson wrote about a mock trial held by the crew of Thomas

PIRATES ENJOYING THEMSELVES AT SEA

Anstis, who at one time sailed with Bartholomew Roberts.

The president (judge) sat in a tree with a
piece of canvas, looking like a judge's robe,
draped over his shoulders. He had large glasses
perched on his nose and a shaggy cap on his
head.

The register read the charges to the defendant. The defendant pleaded "not guilty," say-
ing he had been forced to become a pirate. The
president shouted that the prisoner was a
"lousy, pitiful, ill-looked DOG" and should be in
"the sun, drying like a scarecrow," which
meant the accused looked guilty and deserved
to hang.

The register called witnesses to testify. One
person after another shouted insults at each
other. The trial wore on and on. Finally, the
president interrupted the attorney general to
ask if dinner was ready. The attorney general
answered, "Yes, my lord."

The president then declared the defendant
guilty because: 1) He felt someone should be
hanged, 2) the defendant looked like he should
be hanged, and 3) the president was hungry
and wanted his dinner. The mock trial then

broke up, and everyone, including the prisoner, went to dinner.

Not all mock trials were funny. In one, the defendant got so upset he threw a hand grenade at the jury and sliced off the arm of the attorney general with his cutlass.

Whichever way it was, the mock trial enabled pirates to prepare themselves for what might happen if they were captured. It was also an exciting way for the men to pass long boring hours after careening their ship.

"Jolly Roger" was the name given to pirate flags. Some people think that the name came from "Old Roger," an English name for the devil. Others think it came from "joli rouge," "pretty red" in French. The first buccaneers living in the West Indies flew red flags atop their ships. Later, the black flag with a white design became popular. Each ship had its own emblem, or symbol, and every one was meant to strike terror in the hearts of merchant crews.

Most Jolly Rogers portrayed skeletons (the symbol of death), daggers, cutlasses, and bleeding hearts. Around 1700, Emanuel Wynne, the

French pirate, flew one of the first Jolly Rogers with a skull and crossbones above an hourglass. That symbol warned his prey that time was running out.

Thomas Tew's Jolly Roger had a white arm waving a dagger; Calico Jack Rackham's, a white skull with two crossed cutlasses beneath it. Christopher Moody's was red with a white arm waving a dagger, a yellow skull and crossbones, and a yellow hourglass. Edward Low's was black with a red skeleton, and Blackbeard's was black with a white skeleton, which had horns and a tail like the devil. In its hand was an hourglass, and beneath the devil's pitchfork tail were bloody red hearts.

Pirates wanted their nicknames, ships' names, and Jolly Rogers to be known and feared by the rest of the world.

A JOLLY ROGER—
A PIRATE SHIP'S FLAG.
MOST JOLLY ROGERS
HAD SYMBOLS OF
DEATH ON THEM.

❖ 3 ❖

BUCCANEERS, PIRATES, AND PRIVATEERS

During the late 1500's, the first French, Dutch, and British *buccaneers* lived on Hispaniola. They slaughtered wild cattle and hogs and were called "boucaniers," because they roasted "boucan" to sell to the ships' crews. The Spanish hated these men and ran them off the island after killing their animals.

The boucaniers moved to Tortuga, a small island north of Hispaniola. In revenge, they attacked Spanish ships and settlements. This was the beginning of piracy in the West Indies. Those who captured and plundered ships for themselves eventually became known as "pirates."

Soon after the British captured Jamaica in 1655, many English pirates from Tortuga moved to Port Royal across the bay from Kingston. It was also a base for British *privateers*.

When Britain was at war, there weren't enough warships in the Royal Navy, so private vessels, or privateers, were commissioned by the government to capture and plunder enemy ships. Privateers, unlike pirates, gave part of their plunder to the King.

PORT ROYAL, JAMAICA, HOME BASE TO MANY
PIRATES IN THE SEVENTEENTH CENTURY

Not all people living in Port Royal were pirates or privateers. Many were tradesmen such as cabinetmakers, tailors, and painters. Also, there were numerous taverns, punch houses, and brothels in the bustling port city.

A London reporter described Port Royal at that time as "The dunghill of the universe, the refuse of all creation, as sickly as a hospital, as dangerous as the plague, as hot as hell, and as wicked as the devil."

Port Royal stayed this way until June 7, 1692, the day of the terrible earthquake and tidal wave. The earth shook violently, then opened up, and swallowed almost everything except a paltry ten acres of land. The succeeding tidal wave swept more people, animals, and buildings out to sea. Over two thousand people lost their lives. Nine out of ten houses and three forts were destroyed.

Shortly afterward, the last of the English pirates from Tortuga and those who survived the Port Royal earthquake moved to New Providence Island in the Bahamas.

The Bahamas had hundreds of *cays* and *reefs* surrounded by shallow water where pirates could hide to await their prey or disappear if warships were in the area.

By 1713, this port had become more lawless then Port Royal. People lived in tents and shacks. The harbor was full of rotting ships that could no longer sail. Chickens, pigs, and dogs routed through garbage. Drunks lay about. People fought. People killed. People got sick and died.

In the summer of 1718, Governor Woodes Rogers arrived on New Providence. He brought the King's Pardon, which said that any pirate signing before September 5, 1718, would not be arrested and tried for past crimes. Pardoned pirates would get rewards for capturing unpardoned pirates. Most men readily signed, although many eventually reverted back to their old ways.

Governor Rogers tried to clean up the den of pirates and make New Providence into a successful plantation colony. But most of his attempts at reform were unsuccessful.

Over the years, the number of pirates became fewer, as European governments enforced stronger laws against them. More war-

ships were sent to find and capture them. They were no longer welcome in colonial ports.

By the 1800s, there were even fewer pirates, because the new steam engine was being used in warships and merchantmen. This engine could propel a ship forward or backward, which meant that merchantmen and warships now had the advantage over pirates' sailing ships.

Throughout history, there have always been pirates. Today air pirates hijack airplanes to other countries. Sea pirates hijack power boats to ship illegal drugs. Governments today have waged war against pirates just like governments did over two hundred years ago.

THE BUCCANEER WAS
A COLORFUL FELLOW.

INFAMOUS PIRATES

Blackbeard was the nickname of Edward Teach, one of the most feared pirates to ever sail the seas. He had bushy black hair and eyebrows and a long black beard braided with colorful ribbons. When attacking ships, Blackbeard had a brace of pistols slung across his shoulders as well as a cutlass in his belt. He often tucked fuses of hemp cord, dipped in saltpeter and lime water, under the brim of his hat. When lit, smoke drifted around his head making him look like the devil.

Blackbeard was known for his daring deeds. It is said that he mixed gunpowder with rum, set it on fire, and then gulped down the whole concoction. His men feared him. And unlike most pirate captains, he had total control of his crew.

On November 22, 1718, Lieutenant Maynard, the commander of two warships, at-

BLACKBEARD'S APPEARANCE AND THE STORIES
TOLD ABOUT HIM MADE EVERYONE FEAR HIM.

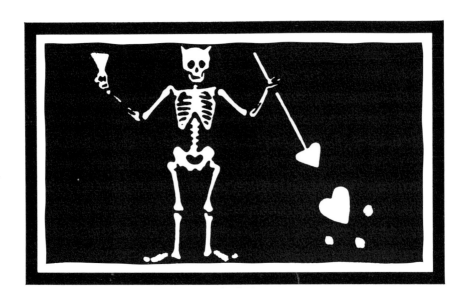

BLACKBEARD'S JOLLY ROGER

tacked Blackbeard's vessel off Ocracoke Island, North Carolina. The pirates fired a huge broadside, crippling Maynard's ships and killing twenty-nine men.

Whooping and hollering, Blackbeard and his men swung aboard Maynard's vessel. Unexpectedly, soldiers swarmed out of the ship's hold. Pandemonium broke out. Pistols cracked. Cutlasses clanked. The deck became slippery with blood as each man fought for his life.

The soldiers fired their pistols at Blackbeard. He cut down one man after another. Lieutenant Maynard aimed point-blank at Blackbeard and fired. Blackbeard drew his cutlass. Maynard did the same. With a furious clank, Blackbeard snapped Maynard's cutlass in half. Maynard grabbed his pistol and fired again.

Blackbeard, with his cutlass raised, moved in for the kill. A soldier aimed his pistol at Blackbeard's throat and fired. Blood spurted everywhere. But Blackbeard fought on.

Shooting and stabbing, the soldiers closed in. At last, Blackbeard fell. Lieutenant Maynard ordered Blackbeard's head cut off and hung from the bowsprit of his ship. His body was thrown overboard. A legend is told that when it hit the water, it swam around and around the ship before sinking.

BLACKBEARD DIED OF FIVE PISTOL SHOTS AND TWENTY DEEP CUTS AROUND HIS BODY. HIS HEAD WAS HUNG FROM THE BOWSPRIT OF HIS SHIP.

Lieutenant Maynard wrote in his report that Blackbeard died with five pistol shots and twenty deep cuts about his body.

Bartholomew Roberts was a merchant who had been captured by pirates. When the pirate captain and several of his men were killed in an ambush, Bartholomew led the pirates to safety and was elected to replace the dead captain.

Several weeks after taking command, Bartholomew and his men came upon a fleet of forty-two Portuguese treasure galleons and two warships anchored off the coast of Brazil.

The pirates sailed alongside the most heavily-laden ship and fired a broadside. Before the smoke had cleared, everyone swung aboard the vessel and captured her.

Bartholomew and his men outran the pursuing warships. On board the *prize*, the pirates found furs, hogsheads (barrels) of sugar and tobacco, jewels, and 40,000 gold moidores ($130,000). Bartholomew kept a diamond-studded gold cross that had been meant for the king of Portugal.

BARTHOLOMEW ROBERTS WAS BORN IN WALES IN 1682. NOT VERY MUCH IS KNOWN ABOUT HIS LIFE.

Weeks later, Bartholomew and his men escaped warships from Barbados and Martinique. The pirates hated anyone coming from these ports, so they made a new Jolly Roger. It showed a pirate standing on two skulls. Underneath were the letters "ABH" and "AMA," which stood for "A Barbadian Head" and "A Martiniquian Head."

On February 5, 1722, Bartholomew's three ships were anchored in Cape Lopez, West Africa, when Captain Chaloner Ogle, commander of the warship *Swallow*, sighted the pirates he had been sent to capture.

Bartholomew thought the *Swallow* was a merchantman and sent the *Ranger* after her. She headed for open seas. Out of sight of the harbor, Ogle ordered his men to attack. Ten pirates were killed and twenty wounded before surrendering.

Ogle returned to Cape Lopez for the remaining pirates. Bartholomew saw the warship and ordered the *Royal Fortune* to sail for the open seas. Then he went to his cabin and dressed in a red damask suit with a black *tricorne* and red feather. He slipped the diamond-studded Portuguese cross around his neck and slung a brace of pistols over his shoulders.

Back on deck, Bartholomew saw the *Swallow* heading straight for the pirates. The soldiers fired a broadside, toppling the *Fortune's mizzenmast.*

ROBERTS WITH TWO OF HIS SHIPS, THE *ROYAL FORTUNE* AND *RANGER* (IN BACKGROUND)

But when the smoke had cleared, Bartholomew was slumped over a cannon. He had been killed. The pirates heaved their captain, dressed in all his finery, overboard.

Bartholomew Roberts, a strict disciplinarian, never drank liquor, only tea, and held religious services on board ship. In four years he and his men had captured and plundered more than 400 ships.

Most people have not heard about *Samuel Bellamy*. At least not until 1982, when Barry Clifford, a former high school teacher, found the wreck of Bellamy's ship off Cape Cod, Massachusetts.

Since the discovery of the *Whydah*, divers have brought up navigational instruments, pottery, gold, and cannons worth millions of dollars. The *Whydah* is the only pirate vessel that has ever been salvaged. Someday Mr. Clifford hopes to build a museum to show what it was like being a pirate in the eighteenth century.

When Samuel Bellamy and his men captured the *Whydah*, it was loaded with silver,

THE *WHYDAH*, SAMUEL BELLAMY'S SHIP, THE WRECK
OF WHICH WAS FOUND OFF CAPE COD, MASSACHUSETTS,
IN 1982 BY BARRY CLIFFORD. THE SHIP WAS UNDER
THIRTY FEET OF WATER AND FIFTEEN FEET OF SAND.

AN ARTIST'S RENDERING OF BELLAMY

gold, ivory, jewels, sugar, indigo, and Jesuit's bark (used to treat malaria).

Off the Atlantic coast of the colonies, the *Whydah* pirates captured a sloop commanded by a Captain Beer. After taking the cargo, Bellamy wanted to return the ship. But the crew was against it.

Bellamy, known as an orator, shouted at Beer, "Damn my blood! I'm sorry they won't let you have your sloop. Damn the sloop! We must sink her. And she could have been of use to you. Though you are a SNEAKING PUPPY, and so are those who submit to rich men's laws for their own security. The COWARDLY DOGS have not the courage to defend what they get by being knaves. Damn them for being crafty rascals, and you for being a HEN-HEARTED NUMBSKULL. . . ."

The speech went on and on. Finally, the pirates sunk Beer's sloop and put the prisoners ashore on Block Island, Rhode Island.

On April 26, 1717, Samuel and his men were sailing between Nantucket shoals and George's Bank, Massachusetts, when they captured the *Mary Anne*, a sloop from Virginia.

THE *MARY ANNE*. FIVE OF HER CREW MEMBERS
WERE HANGED IN BOSTON AS PIRATES IN 1717.

Shortly before sunset, the ships sailed into a thick fog. By ten o'clock, they had lost sight of one another. Soon afterwards, the *Mary Anne* ran aground near Cape Cod, Massachusetts.

The next morning, two colonists brought her sailors ashore. The men of the *Whydah* weren't as lucky. Their vessel had broken up, and only two were able to swim through the crashing waves to safety.

Six of Bellamy's men were tried in Boston on October 22, 1717 and hanged. No one knows how many pirates drowned and how many escaped. Soon after the wreck, nineteen were seen plundering ships off Cape Ann, Massachusetts. Samuel Bellamy was never seen again.

There were probably a number of women who sailed on pirate ships. But *Mary Read* and *Anne Bonny* were the most famous, because they were captured and brought to trial.

Mary, born in England, was dressed in boy's clothes from the time she was a toddler. When she was in her teens, she worked as a boy servant, then joined the infantry and later the cavalry fighting in the War of the Spanish Succession (1701–1714).

While in the cavalry, Mary fell in love with her tentmate, a Dutch soldier. She admitted to him that she was a woman. Soon the young

couple were married, and Mary wore women's clothes for the first time.

Honorably discharged from the army, the newlyweds moved to Breda, in the Netherlands, and opened a public house. Soon after, Mary's husband died. She closed the pub, once again dressed in men's clothes, and reenlisted in the infantry. About this time the war ended, so Mary deserted and signed aboard a merchant-man sailing for the West Indies.

In the Atlantic Ocean, the ship was attacked by pirates and Mary joined the outlaws. She sailed with them a few months before settling down in the notorious pirate haven on New Providence Island, Bahamas. There, Mary signed the King's Pardon, absolving herself from past acts of piracy. But eventually she became a pirate again.

WHEN SHE WAS THIRTEEN,
MARY READ RAN AWAY
AND SIGNED ABOARD A
ROYAL NAVY WARSHIP.

It was during this time that she met Anne Bonny, a beautiful Irish girl from Charleston, South Carolina. Anne's father was a lawyer and rich plantation owner.

When Anne was sixteen, she eloped to New Providence Island with James Bonny, a sailor. But she eventually left him for the notorious pirate Calico Jack Rackham.

When Anne and Mary met, Anne thought Mary was a boy and began to flirt with her. Mary was forced to tell Anne her secret. Immediately, the two women became friends. Calico Jack, thinking Mary was a man, became jealous, so the women were forced to tell him the truth.

Months later, Mary fell in love with a young prisoner captured from a merchantman. After sailing with the pirates a few weeks, the young

AS A YOUNG GIRL, ANNE
BONNY LEARNED HOW
TO SHOOT A PISTOL AND
THROW A KNIFE.

man had an argument with one of the men who challenged him to a duel. Mary, afraid he would be killed, picked a fight with the same pirate. Then, she cunningly challenged him to an earlier duel.

Mary and the pirate fought furiously with pistols and cutlasses. Mary at last saw her opportunity and stabbed the pirate. He fell dead at her feet. Now a hero, Mary admitted to everyone she was really a woman. A short time later, Mary and her man were married.

In October 1720 near Negril Point, Jamaica, the pirates were captured by Captain Barnet and taken to trial at St. Jago de la Vega, Jamaica. Calico Jack and eight crewmembers were found guilty of piracy and hanged. Mary and Anne were also found guilty, but both pleaded "quick with child" (pregnant).

The court did not want to hang mothers to be, so they were returned to their cell. A few

PIRATES SOMETIMES
FOUGHT OVER WHO
WOULD BE CAPTAIN
OF THE SHIP.

CALICO JACK RACKHAM

ANNE BONNY AND MARY READ WERE TRIED AND
CONVICTED OF PIRACY IN 1720. ACCORDING TO THE
RECORDS OF ONE WITNESS AT THE TRIAL, THE TWO
WOMEN "WORE MEN'S JACKETS, LONG TROUSERS,
AND HANDKERCHIEFS TIED AROUND THEIR HEADS."

months later Mary became ill and died. No one knows what happened to Anne. But it is certain she did not hang.

Very few pirates retired rich and lived to old age. Pirates either died of disease, like Mary Read; in battle, like Blackbeard and Bartholomew Roberts; in a shipwreck, like Samuel Bellamy; or on the end of a hangman's noose, like Calico Jack Rackham.

 GLOSSARY

Barnacles: a hard-shelled sea animal that grows on the hull of a ship

Buccaneers: another name for pirates

Careen: to clean and repair the hull of a ship

Cat-o'-nine-tails: a whip with nine pieces of knotted cord attached to a handle

Cays: tiny islands

Cooper: barrelmaker

Cutlass: a short, heavy curved sword

Galleons: sailing vessel used for war or commerce

Gibbet: post

Gunwales: railings at the side of the ship

Jolly Roger: a flag with each pirate ship's particular emblem

Merchantmen: trading ships

Mizzenmast: the mast aft of the main mast

Privateer: crew member of an armed private ship commissioned to cruise against enemy ships

Prize: captured ship

Reef: a ridge of rocks or sand at or near the surface of the water

Shoot a broadside: all cannons on one side of the ship firing together

Tricorne: a three-cornered hat

◆ BIBLIOGRAPHY ◆

Botting, Douglas. *The Pirates.* New York: Time-Life Books, 1978. Mr. Botting used consultants and contributors who were professors and curators of museums, both American and British. The first contributor he lists under "acknowledgments" is Hugh Rankin, a history professor at Tulane University (New Orleans). Professor Rankin has written several books on pirates. Two are listed below.

Dow, George Frances and Edmonds, John Henry. *The Pirates of the New England Coast 1630-1730.* Mr. Dow was curator of the Society for the Preservation of New England Antiquities. Mr. Edmonds was Massachusetts State Archivist.

Lee, Robert E., Ph.D. *Blackbeard The Pirate: a Reappraisal of His Life and Times.* Winston-Salem, North Carolina: John F. Blair Publishers, 1974. Dr. Lee is retired Dean of the Law School at Wake Forest University (North Carolina) and has published numerous law books before *Blackbeard.*

Lydon, James G. *Pirates, Privateers, and Profits.* Upper Saddle River, NJ: the Gregg Press, 1970. The introduction to this book is by Richard B. Morris, Professor of History of Columbia University. Mr. Lydon graduated from Harvard University and Columbia. He was a Professor of History at Duquesne University (Pittsburgh) when he wrote this book.

Rankin, Hugh F. *The Pirates of Colonial North Carolina.* Department of Cultural Resources, North Carolina Division of Archives and History, 1960; 1984 reprint. As of 1984, Dr. Rankin was Professor of History at Tulane University. He has also written *The Golden Age of Piracy,* Holt, Rinehart, and Winston, 1969. He was a contributor of *The Pirates,* Time-Life, 1978.

Sherry, Frank. *Raiders and Rebels: the Golden Age of Piracy.* New York: William Morrow & Co., 1986. Mr. Sherry is a journalist and has won several prestigious awards for his journalism.

The author obtained copies of trial transcripts for Captain William Kidd, Calico Jack Rackham, Mary Read, and Anne Bonny from Dr. Robert E. Lee and the Institute of Jamaica in Kingston, Jamaica.

FOR FURTHER READING

Larranaga, Robert D. *Pirates and Buccaneers*. Minneapolis: Lerner, 1970.

Marrin, Albert. *The Sea Rovers: Pirates, Privateers, and Buccaneers*. New York: Atheneum, 1984.

McCall, Edith. *Pirates and Privateers*. Chicago: Children's Press, 1963.

Thompson, Brenda and Rosemary Giesen. *Pirates*. Minneapolis: Lerner, 1974.

Yolen, Jane. *Pirates in Petticoats*. New York: David McKay, 1963.

◆ INDEX ◆

Page numbers in italics indicate illustrations.